A SIENA BOOK

Siena is an imprint of Parragon Books
Published by Parragon Book Service Ltd,
Units 13 - 17, Avonbridge Trading Estate,
Atlantic Road, Avonmouth, Bristol BS11 9QD

Original concept by Julian Tucki • Improved by Guy Parr
Developed by Caroline Repchuk and Dug Steer

Produced by The Templar Company plc,
Pippbrook Mill, London Road, Dorking, Surrey RH4 1JE

Edited by Caroline Repchuk
Designed by Janie Louise Hunt

Printed and bound in Italy

ISBN 0-75251-308-7

BIG BAMBOO'S
Blackcurrant
Birthday

ILLUSTRATED BY STEPHANIE BOEY

WRITTEN BY DUGALD STEER

SIENA

Big Bamboo was such a lazy panda.
He always woke up late.
One morning he woke up very late indeed.
As he lay dozing he thought he heard a
noise coming from downstairs.
What was all that banging and clattering?
"Oh, no!" said Big Bamboo. "Work!"

Big Bamboo didn't like work at all. He much preferred eating. He climbed out of bed and got dressed. Then he crept downstairs on tiptoes, (*which for a big panda like him was not easy!*), and sneaked out of the house.

He was going to find somewhere to hide
so he wouldn't have to work!

He didn't realise the other Jam Pandas had heard him.
They were looking at each other, smiling.

Little did Big Bamboo know that
the 'work' was all for him!
He wasn't very good at remembering
things, (*unless, of course, it was where his
secret jam supply was hidden!*) and had
forgotten that today was his birthday.
But the other Jam Pandas had remembered,
and now they were secretly preparing a
special birthday party just for him.

11

They worked hard all morning, and at last everything was ready.

The cottage had been decorated with balloons, and the table was covered with jam sandwiches, jam sponges and even jam jelly!

There were party hats and a lot of presents.

Grandma Jam knew what Big Bamboo's favourite present would be – a specially big pot of delicious blackcurrant jam!

All they needed now was Big Bamboo and the party could begin. But where was he? The Jam Pandas set out to look for him. First they looked in the garden.

"He can't be far away," said Ma Jam.

But he wasn't in the garden.
"Perhaps he's in the orchard," said Grandma.

15

Peaches and Plum, the cheeky twins, searched
for Big Bamboo in the orchard.
"I'm sure they'll find him there," said Ma Jam.

But he wasn't in the orchard.
"Perhaps he's in the wood," said Pa.

Pa searched all through the wood but
Big Bamboo wasn't there either.
Just then little Jim Jam, the
baby panda, began crawling away.
"Big Bam! Big Bam!" he said.
"Jumping Jamspoons!" said Grandma.
"That little chap's got an idea!"

Jim Jam was heading straight for the blackcurrant patch.
In no time at all he had disappeared
amongst the bushes.

Peaches and Plum were not far behind him.
"Look!" they shouted, pointing
excitedly at the blackcurrant patch.
"It's Big Bamboo!"

Big Bamboo loved blackcurrants.
They were his very favourite fruit of all.
He had been hiding there all morning
and he had eaten nearly every blackcurrant
in the patch! Now he looked like
a very poorly panda indeed.
"Ooooh!" he groaned.
"My tummy hurts!"

Back at the cottage, Big Bamboo
went straight to bed.
"Ooooh!" he groaned again.
"What a birthday!"
Grandma set to work at once and prepared
a pot of her special medicinal jam.
Before long Big Bamboo was feeling much
better, but he was very disappointed
that he had missed his party, and
spoiled his big surprise.
"I'm very sorry," he told the others.
"I'll try not to be so greedy in future."

The next day he got up, went downstairs and... Surprise!

HAPPY BIRTHDAY BIG BAMBOO!

The Jam Pandas had decided that Big Bamboo had suffered enough for his greediness, and to hold the party a day late. Besides, it would be terrible to waste all those lovely jam sandwiches!

• **T H E   E N D** •